With best wishes of
Mary Marsh Buff
and
Conrad Buff

HAH-NEE

of the Cliff Dwellers

Mary and Conrad Buff

1956

HOUGHTON MIFFLIN COMPANY, BOSTON

The Riverside Press, Cambridge

LIBRARY OF CONGRESS CATALOGUE CARD NUMBER 56-8268
PRINTED IN U.S.A.

CONTENTS

The author wishes to thank the following persons for their kind help in collecting material about the Cliffdwellers: Mr. Don Watson, of the Mesa Verde National Park, Mesa Verde, Colorado; Dr. Frederick W. Hodge, Dr. M. H. Harrington, and Mrs. E. L. Robinson, of the Southwest Museum of Los Angeles.

PROLOGUE

In safe caverns they lived
The ancient cliff dwellers
Where now four states
Come together
Utah
Arizona
Colorado
And New Mexico

A land of high mountains
A land of dry deserts
A land of deep canyons
A rugged land

Upon green tablelands
The cliff Indians planted corn
They snared rabbits and birds
And shot deer and bear
With bow and arrow

Thus
For years and years
They lived
Safe in their rocky houses
A happy Stone Age people

Then
Slowly late in the thirteenth century
Came years of dryness

When summer rains were few
And winter snows were scarce
When springs dried up
And storage jars grew empty
Of corn
And water

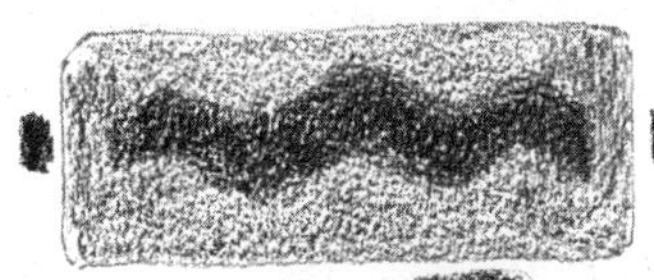

And a great drought settled upon the land
For twenty-four bitter years

As the rains failed
As springs slowly dried up
The Indians grew thirsty
And hungry
Angry and frightened
They —
Who seldom quarreled —
Quarreled with each other
Man against his neighbor
Clan against clan

Fearing each other
They feared their gods more
Had not their gods forsaken them?
Were not their gods angry?
What had the people done?
What had they not done?

Thus
Year after year
As the land grew dry
As a whitened bone

The Indians left their safe cliffs
And wandered away
South and southeast
Hoping to find a land
Where rain fell
And corn grew tall once more

This is their story
The story of the vanished cliff dwellers

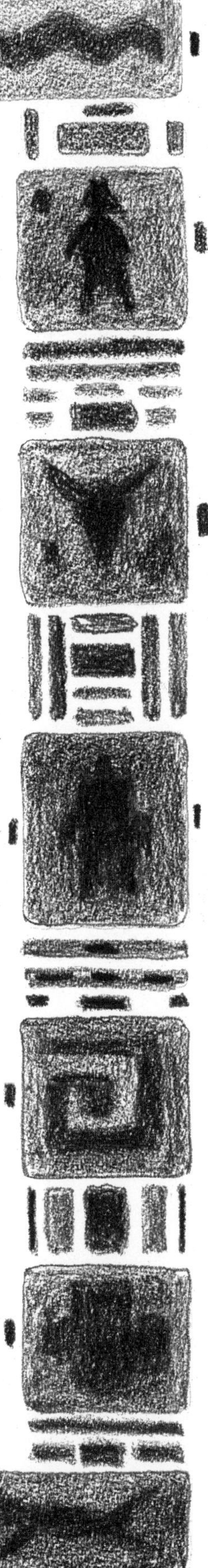

CHAPTER ONE

HAH-NEE AT THE SPRING

HAH-NEE, the Indian boy, slipped through the door of his stone hut built on a ledge of rock along the face of a high cliff. Mozo, his dog, jumped after him. It was cold and unfriendly on the terrace, for dawn had not yet come. Hah-nee hugged his turkey-feather robe about him as he crouched on the cold stone floor. Across the narrow canyon, under a large overhanging ledge, was the Great City where several hundred Indians had once lived together in stone houses they and their forefathers had built. Now, there were not so many living there. People had been leaving over the years because of a long drought. The corn grew thin and parched, and many water jars were empty. None of the vanished people ever returned, and no one knew just where they had gone.

Hah-nee watched the fires flicker here and there in firepits beside stone walls in the Cliff City. Turkeys caged at the rear of the stone huts called, "Gobble gobble," to get out. Children

laughed and shouted as they chased each other in and out of the houses, trying to keep warm. Women knelt before stone metates, singing, as they ground corn into meal for breakfast cakes.

Suddenly, as it grew lighter, Hah-nee heard a flute player welcoming the rising sun. A hunter climbed up to the flat-topped mesa, clinging with his strong toes to the carved toe holds in the face of the slippery rocks. From many round underground kivas before stone homes came sounds of singing men. Priests and many men spent all night in the kivas, where it was warm. They prayed for rain and sang old chants. They told stories, slept, and talked together. The kivas were both churches and clubhouses for men and older boys.

Then, as Hah-nee heard someone wheezing and coughing nearby, he knew Wupa was awake. Wupa lived in a small cliff-dwelling which was like a storehouse. He was the oldest Indian living anywhere in the cliffs. Wupa, the Great, some people called him. Even though he was toothless, almost blind, and stiff with age, he was still wise old Wupa. He knew more about the far-off happy days of his people than any other man. Many Indians asked him to judge their disputes. He was always calm and fair. Even ten-year-old Hah-nee talked with Wupa when he was troubled. Wupa listened to him as if he were a grown man. So Hah-nee loved the old Indian as much as he loved Mother Nuva, his Father, or Uncle Osa.

Wupa had a strange pet, a large black raven called Kisha. When Wupa was a boy, he found Kisha, then a fledgling, under a tree. The two had grown old together. Ravens live to be very,

very old. Kisha never left Wupa except when he hunted for food. Some of the Indians of the cliffs were afraid of ravens, especially Kisha, but they trusted Wupa so much that they never hurt the great black bird.

Hah-nee threw dry wood on the smoldering fire in the fire-pit and placed a clay bowl of cornmeal mush on a flat stone griddle over it. Soon the fire would warm the rock and then the mush. He would take warm mush to Wupa. Then he slipped a gourd held by a yucca fiber over his shoulder and climbed downward, placing his toes carefully in the toe holds. I'll get fresh water at the spring, he thought. Mozo, afraid of the steep cliffs, waited for Hah-nee to return.

It was still dark in the narrow canyon as Hah-nee crept down the well-worn trail. Near the bottom of the canyon he saw the sky reflected in the pool. There *was* water. He let the gourd slide into the pool. Then, as he pulled it up, he heard a rustle in the bushes. Suddenly a stone whizzed past his head. Someone shouted:

"Hah-nee's a FUNNY HEAD . . . Hah-nee's a FUNNY HEAD . . . Hah-nee's evil."

Hah-nee stood still. Why should anyone call him a FUNNY HEAD? It was bad luck to call anyone "evil." Hah-nee was puzzled.

"Hah-nee's a Ute," yelled another. The Utes were nomadic warriors, greatly feared by the people of the cliffs. Utes stole women and children. Utes stole corn. Utes killed peaceful farmers. It was because of the Utes that the cliff dwellers had built

their safe cliff houses many years ago. Another stone whizzed by. Another voice shouted, "Hah-nee's a Ute. Funny-Head Hah-nee."

The bushes rustled again. Hah-nee heard sounds of running feet. He was frightened. How did one fight those who threw stones in the darkness? He ran up the trail and his heart beat twice as fast as usual. Who could those be? Were they boys of the Coyote Clan, who were always fighting? He knew that the people of his clan, the Antelope Clan, and the people of the Coyote Clan were not friendly. He did not know why. Something had happened between them years and years ago. Since that time, the clan people disliked each other. His mother had told him this.

The mush was warm. Hah-nee carried the bowl carefully as he climbed to Wupa's ledge. The old man, covered with a brown bear robe, was sitting in his cold one-room cell. As he heard Hah-nee, he opened his slits of eyes, brushing straggling locks of white hair from his face. He had no teeth left. Hah-nee remembered the happy day when Wupa lost his very last tooth. The old man had suffered from toothache for many years. So did all of the older people. Toothache was something the priests could not help. Toothache and stiff backs.

"Grandfather, mush," said Hah-nee. "It will stop your coughing. Fresh water too from the spring."

The old man took the bowl with trembling hands, saying, "Hot mush is good this cold morning. The night was long, Hah-nee. My old bones ache with the chill."

Wupa was so stiff with age that he had not left his cell for years and years. Hah-nee smiled as he watched him dip two skinny fingers into the mush and lick them eagerly.

"Where is Kisha?" Hah-nee asked.

"Kisha? Out hunting. He will come home after the sun rises. Do you know what he has been up to now? He has hidden my brown bag with the red string. I don't know where, either. Kisha thinks stealing and hiding things are very funny games. They are not funny to me, with my old eyes," said the old man.

"Kisha loves bright colors, so he must have liked the red string about the bag," added Hah-nee thoughtfully.

"We must find it, Hah-nee, you and I. There is something in it I must have," mumbled Wupa. "I *must* find it. You look for it, Hah-nee. You have keen young eyes."

Hah-nee peered in the crevices of Wupa's house where Kisha usually hid things. He found a piece of dried chipmunk fur, a red berry, a shiny arrowhead, and a piece of white rock. But not one trace of the bag. Kisha loved to dig holes in the sand and hide things, then cover the hole with sand and leaves. Hah-nee looked for a telltale mound, but he could find nothing.

"Nothing, Grandfather, nothing at all," he said.

"Well, Kisha will soon be back. Maybe we can get him to find the bag. I am sure he took it. No one has been here since yesterday. Yesterday I had it in my hand," continued the old Indian. As they were talking, in swooped black, shiny Kisha, lighting on a rock, a dead field mouse dangling from his bill. He laid the mouse at his master's feet as if to say, Your breakfast, Master, look what I caught just for you. He cocked his black head and looked wise.

"Kisha," scolded Hah-nee. "Kisha, where did you hide

Wupa's bag with the red string? You know what I mean, Kisha. Where is it?"

But Kisha only stared down at the dead mouse at his master's feet. Then when Wupa did not touch the mouse, Kisha grabbed it and slowly tore it to pieces, eating every bit.

"Grandfather, *you* ask Kisha where the bag is," said Hah-nee. "He understands every word you say to him."

"He understands only what he *wants* to understand," answered Wupa, smiling. "His greatest fun is to tease old Wupa."

Kisha tucked his head under his wing and slept. Silently Wupa and Hah-nee sat on the terrace enjoying the warm morning sunshine. Then Hah-nee, remembering the boys at the spring, said:

"Grandfather, when I was at the spring before dawn, something strange happened."

"Strange? What do you mean, son?" queried the old man.

"Some boys from the Great City threw rocks at me. They called me names. They called me HAH-NEE THE EVIL ONE and HAH-NEE FUNNY HEAD. Then they ran away in the darkness. Why did they do that, Grandfather?"

"They were only teasing you, Hah-nee. You know how you and all children like to scare others in the darkness. Were they boys of the Coyote Clan?"

"I do not know, Grandfather, who they were. Perhaps they were of the Coyote Clan. You know how those people are."

"Yes I do," answered Wupa. "It is too bad people of the same blood are always quarreling. For years it has been so."

"But Grandfather, once I saw myself in a pool of clear water. Then I saw my face was long and my head was not flat behind. Why is that?" asked Hah-nee, looking at the old man.

Wupa smiled as he said, "Don't worry, Hah-nee. The children were only teasing. They like to tease anyone who looks a little different. You *are* taller than they. You can run faster too. You are quick with the bow. Perhaps Mother Nuva did not tie you to the hard cradleboard when you were a baby as did all of the other mothers. So your head did not flatten behind."

"But Grandfather, the boys called me a Ute. I am of our own clan, not of the enemy that steals and kills."

"So you are, Hah-nee. And a good hunter with feet like the wind. First in games, I hear."

The two Indians sat quietly on the warm bearskin rug, enjoying being together. Hah-nee heard his mother grinding corn, and saw the smoke of the fire. When he smelled corn cakes baking on the stone griddle, he arose.

"Grandfather, I go now. When the sun drops I will bring warm mush to you before you sleep."

"Go, son," said Wupa. Kisha cawed goodbye. "The black bird will be with me. Do not think of the children and their taunts. They are only teasing."

CHAPTER TWO

HAH-NEE GOES HUNTING

HAH-NEE felt comforted as he climbed down to his ledge. Uncle Osa and Father had already eaten. Mother Nuva handed Hah-nee some hot corn cakes, saying to her husband, "If it would only rain. There is not one solid water jar left. All are chipped or cracked. I should make new ones. The walls of the house need a new coat of mud. But there is no extra water to do this, unless it rains as it used to rain in the good old days."

"The wind is from the east, Nuva, and moist this morning. We prayed all night in the kiva for rain. Perhaps the gods will hear us," said Father hopefully.

"Wupa has said that when he was young the corn grew as tall as my head," added Hah-nee. "The squash was big and the pods on the vines were full of beans. Many were the nuts on the piñon pines. The yucca was tall too, and full of pods."

"So it was," sighed Uncle Osa. "I remember too, though I am not as old as Wupa. But such times may come again, who knows?"

"The women at the spring this morning said that the priests in the City drove old Honani away yesterday. They warned her never to come back. They say she is a witch. No rain falls because of her and her evil doings," whispered Mother Nuva.

"Old Honani," said Uncle Osa. "She has always been as a child. When her clan people went away because of the drought, they did not take her, for they knew she could not travel with them for long. She is so old. Often I see her wandering alone on the mesa, mumbling to herself and looking everywhere for something. She *is* strange, but I wonder if she is really a witch. She has always been strange, even before the drought," said Uncle Osa softly.

"The priests say so," said Mother Nuva firmly, "and they know. They must find out who is causing the long drought. It must be *someone*. Last spring they said it was Zoni. The spring before that, the flute player with the humped back. The priests drove them away too and they never came back. Still it does not rain.'"

Hah-nee trembled. Father and Mother's words chilled him like a cold wind. Could it be that some people thought *he* might be evil? They had called him the queer one, the one with the strange head. Feeling very unhappy, he arose and took his bow and arrow and his snares from under his sleeping mat. He wanted to be alone for a while and think about things.

"Hah-nee, we go to the field today to clear the weeds and repair the walls in the gully. Will you come with us?" asked Father.

"Father, I would rather hunt for a rabbit or a prairie dog, for we need meat," said the son.

"Well, very well, son, if you wish. But soon now we need you to help with planting and guarding the fields."

"Yes, Father, I will help," said Hah-nee.

"Where do you go to hunt, Hah-nee?" asked Mother Nuva.

"Far on the mesa, Mother, where the rabbits hide."

"Then I will go with you for a while," she said. "I go in search of wild onions, sage, and roots to flavor the stew and mush."

She slipped a large carrying basket on her back, held by a band across her forehead. Father and Uncle disappeared, their long digging sticks over their shoulders. Hah-nee and his mother climbed upward, and Mozo found a roundabout way to the top of the flat mesa scattered with cornfields and low brush.

"It feels like rain," said Mother Nuva, looking at the white clouds rising from the eastern horizon. "Perhaps I will find some beeweed this morning," she said hopefully. "Then I will boil it down and make black paint. If it *does* rain and there is water, I can mold some new jars. The paint will be ready."

Mother Nuva loved to make jars of clay, but even more to decorate them. She was one of the best potters living in the cliff dwellings. Her jars were the envy of many other women. She was thinking of the designs she would paint on the new jars as she trudged along, looking everywhere for weeds, berries, and roots. She knew them all. She had learned about them from her mother.

Hah-nee glanced back at the Great City under its vast rocky roof. It seemed already small, hidden in deep shadow. Soon he

could not see it at all.

"Mother," he said suddenly, feeling very close to her, "At the spring before dawn some boys shouted evil names at me and threw stones."

"Names? What names?" asked Mother Nuva in a strange voice.

"Oh bad names. They called me FUNNY-HEAD, HAH-NEE THE EVIL ONE and HAH-NEE THE UTE."

"They did!" exclaimed Mother Nuva.

"Then they ran away and I do not know who they were," added Hah-nee.

Mother Nuva muttered something under her breath, but Hah-nee could not hear her.

"What did you say, Mother?" he asked.

"Oh, nothing, son. Nothing. The children have been listening to idle talk around the fire. Maybe they were of the Coyote Clan, those lazy people. Always gossiping. Their cornfield is near ours, and they envy us our crops. Father and Uncle Osa work so hard. Every time we get a good crop the Coyote people are jealous. But then," she sighed, "people say and do strange things when times are bad, as they now are. Many people are hungry."

"I told Grandfather Wupa about the boys," said Hah-nee.

"You told Wupa? What did he say?"

"He only said that they were teasing me and to forget about it. But my head is *not* as the others, Mother!" exclaimed Hah-nee, feeling the back of his head.

"It is all an old, old story, Hah-nee," said Mother Nuva

sadly; "it is a story I thought everyone had forgotten years and years ago. I cannot speak of it now for it hurts me here." She placed her strong brown hand over her heart. "Ask Wupa. He is wiser than I am." She forced a smile as she looked down at him. "Now run on and trap that rabbit for supper, Hah-nee, and pray to the gods that your arrow may be swift and your snares strong. I will search for roots, weeds, and berries to flavor the stew." She left Hah-nee hurriedly and did not look back as she usually did.

He watched her sturdy short figure almost hidden by the huge basket until she disappeared in a little gully. Mozo and Hah-nee were alone on the mesa. Mozo sniffed in the bushes while Hah-nee studied the ground, looking for signs of runs made by rabbits and birds and smaller game. He saw what looked like a well-marked trail and pegged down one small snare made of his mother's hair. He baited it with one kernel of corn. Corn was precious and could not be wasted.

Dog and boy wandered on across the mesa watching and listening to the sights and sounds of the upland country. Hah-nee saw another well-worn run and pegged down another snare. Then, as the sun was hot, he sat under a piñon pine and rested. A lizard scrambled up on a rock to sun himself. A beautiful butterfly fluttered upward through the trees. Hah-nee smelled a skunk. The air was soft and moist. Great white clouds raced through the sky, driven by a wind from the east. Hah-nee prayed to the gods that his arrow might be swift and his snares strong.

Feeling sleepy, Hah-nee lay down. Mozo lay beside him but

his ears and nose were constantly twitching. Suddenly the dog growled gently, and Hah-nee sat up. In the distance he saw a rabbit, its head turned from them, nibbling at the leaves of a bush. As quick as a flash, Hah-nee aimed. The arrow found its mark before the rabbit saw it. How lucky I am today, thought Hah-nee, to get a rabbit so soon. He tied the rabbit's hind legs to his sash with a yucca string and retraced his steps.

When he checked the second snare, the corn was still there and the snare was empty. He rolled it up and put it in his carrying bag. Suddenly Mozo ran ahead barking, his hair standing up along his back. Hah-nee ran after him. As they reached the other snare, a prairie dog was struggling in its meshes. Mozo pounced upon the animal, gave it one sudden jerk, and it was limp. What luck, a rabbit and a prairie dog. Mother would be pleased.

Suddenly the sky clouded over, and black clouds raced across the sky as the wind rose. Calling Mozo, Hah-nee hurried homeward. Mother might not be there yet. If it did rain, he could put out the water jars and perhaps catch some rain water. A few drops of rain fell. In haste he rolled out the water jars, and placed them where water might drip down from the overhanging rocky roof. Across the canyon in the Great City women were looking anxiously at the sky and placing their water jars out to catch rain water. Thunder growled and echoed up and down the canyon, sounding loud and menacing.

Hah-nee, waiting for the rain, climbed up to Wupa's ledge, hoping the old man was not asleep. The thunder had awakened

him, and he was talking to Kisha as Hah-nee crawled up over the ledge.

"Wupa," said Hah-nee happily, "I snared a prairie dog and shot a rabbit on the hunt this morning. When Mother comes home with roots and berries to flavor the stew we will have a good meal. I'll bring you up a soft piece of meat to suck. Did you find the bag?"

"Not yet. I asked Kisha to find it but he only blinked his eyes, cocked his head, looked wise, and went to sleep. I am sure he stole it when I was not looking. But my eyes are so dim I cannot see. He could hide it in front of me and I could not find it."

Hah-nee searched again for the bag, but he could not find it. At last, tired out, he sat quietly beside Grandfather Wupa.

Suddenly he said, "Grandfather, when we were walking over the mesa this morning, Mother Nuva and I, I told her about the boys at the spring, and the bad names they called me. I asked her why the boys did this and she said she could not tell me. It was an old story, she said, and she did not want to talk about it. She said you might tell me because you knew all about it. She said you are wiser than she is."

"She said that?" exclaimed Wupa.

"Yes, Grandfather, she said that," replied Hah-nee.

"Then I will tell you the story, son. But it is a long story, and you must be patient."

"I will," answered Hah-nee uneasily.

CHAPTER THREE

THE SECRET

WUPA coughed, cleared his throat and began: "It was many, many summers ago that this happened. In those days the great dryness had not yet settled upon our land. Gentle 'woman' rains fell always at planting time. Fierce 'man' rains came in the late summer. The roofs of our houses each fall were piled high with yellow and green squash and drying corn. Our storage bins were full to overflowing. The turkeys were fat. Each fall we brought home baskets of piñon nuts to eat during the long cold winter. The hunters were always carrying home mountain sheep, deer, and bear they had shot. It was a glorious time. There was plenty to eat for all of us. No one feared his neighbor as we do now. The gods were kind to us, and we did no wrong."

"Grandfather, I wish I had lived then," sighed Hah-nee, remembering the many times he went to bed hungry and how seldom the crop was good.

"You did live then, Hah-nee, but you lived far away. Three

or four suns' walk from our cliffs. Listen well."

"Tell me, Grandfather," urged the boy with wondering eyes staring at the old man.

"Your father and Uncle Osa," droned Wupa, "as you know, grind and polish digging blades and stone knives that everybody likes to use."

"I know," answered Hah-nee. "The ones that are brown with dark streaks here and there."

"Yes, that stone comes from far away. Each year your father and Uncle made a journey to the place of the stones. It is in enemy country, across a river. Late one fall after the crop was gathered, your father and uncle made the trip. As they were digging out the stones, they heard a sound like that of a baby crying. Both men knew all about the tricks of the enemy, and they thought this was a trick to lure them out and rob them of food and perhaps life. So they hid. But the sound went on and on.

"You know, Hah-nee, how all of our people love children. Many a time I had heard your father and mother complain sadly that they had no sons or daughters to care for them when they grew old. Well, night was at hand. Your father whispered to Uncle Osa, 'That sounds more like a sick or hungry child than a trick of the enemy.' The two men were quiet for a long time listening to the sad cry.

" 'That *must* be a baby,' said your father at last. 'I will find the child.'

" 'Be careful,' warned Uncle Osa. 'You know how clever the enemy is.'

"But your father could stand the cry no longer. He is kind to children, as you know, Hah-nee. He crept silently in the dusk toward a bush from which the sound seemed to come. There, lying on a soft Ute cradleboard, was a fine baby boy. The child was cold and hungry. When your father picked him up, he stopped crying. As he felt your father's arms around him, he smiled. That pleased your father. The boy was large for his age, but thin with hunger."

" 'Where is its mother?' asked Uncle Osa, looking about in the bushes. Finally they found her. She was a young, comely woman, very strong, but she was dead.'

" 'So young a mother,' said Osa sadly. 'Perhaps she was sick. The enemy travels fast after game. Perhaps they could not take a sick woman with them.'

"In the dust they saw tracks of a large party of Utes traveling fast. 'Poor child,' sighed your father. 'If we do not take this baby the coyotes will find him tonight.'

" 'Yes, the coyotes will certainly find him tonight,' said Uncle Osa thoughtfully.

" 'We must take this baby home with us. You know how Nuva has always wanted a son, and so have I. He is a likely child even if he is of the enemy.'

" 'Take him home? What will the people say?' said Uncle Osa, surprised.

" 'The people of the cliffs will not think much about it. People forget soon as they go about their own business. Just another mouth to feed and there is enough food for everybody,'

answered your father. 'After all, children are children, enemy or not.'

"Uncle Osa saw that your father would take the child no matter what he said, so he said no more. But his heart softened too, as the baby smiled at him. The men gathered the stones. Your father carried the baby. They were still afraid of meeting with the enemy, and so they hurried away. In a few days they were home."

"And the baby, was that me?" asked Hah-nee.

"Yes, Hah-nee, the baby was you, or is you now, you big boy," said Wupa fondly.

"That is why I am taller than the other children?"

"Yes, the enemy people are taller than we are," replied his grandfather.

"That is why my face is long and my head round behind?"

"Yes, Hah-nee, that is the reason," answered Wupa gently. "Your mother put you on our hard cradleboard at once," he added, "but your head was already formed and would not change. It was too late. The enemy cradleboard is soft like a pillow, not hard like ours."

"What did Mother say when Father brought home an enemy baby?" asked Hah-nee.

"She was too happy to talk."

"Does anyone remember about this but you, Uncle Osa, Mother, and Father?" he asked again.

"I thought everyone had forgotten all about it. But now that times are bad, someone recalls it. The drought started just

about the time you came to us. The priests have found no way to stop it. Perhaps someone did recall this story," said Wupa thoughtfully.

"They drove Old Honani from the cliffs because she was different," said Hah-nee, thinking hard.

"She was only an old woman with the mind of a child," answered Wupa.

"Yes, but they say she *was* different from the others," replied Hah-nee.

"Yes, she was different," echoed Wupa.

"Wupa, will anything happen to me because I am different—will it?" asked Hah-nee, fear in his voice.

"You, Hah-nee? Of course not. Do not be afraid," said the old man firmly. "Nothing can happen to you. Our clan is greatly respected. While I live no one could possibly hurt you. Or your family either."

Just then the sky seemed to open up and great gusts of rain fell in torrents. Hah-nee hurried down to his home. He moved a jar here or there, trying to catch every drop of precious water. It was a flood, a cloudburst. The canyon echoed thunder many times. It was very frightening. In the Great City people were chanting and laughing and crying with joy at the sudden storm. Soon Hah-nee's black and white jars were half full of rain water. Then, as suddenly as it had come, the rain stopped. The black, life-giving clouds hurried westward.

Mother Nuva hastened down the cliff. She was wet to the skin and breathless, for she had been running. Seeing the water

jars standing on the ledge, half full of water, she smiled and said, "Hah-nee, you *did* get home in time. I hurried fearing you had not returned. The precious water!"

"Mother, I brought home a rabbit and a prairie dog. And when I got home I talked with Wupa. He told me the story of how Father and Uncle Osa found me when I was a baby at the Place of the Stones."

"I am glad he told you, my son. He understands."

"Mother, he says I should not be afraid. Nothing will happen to me."

"Of course nothing will happen to you, Hah-nee, for you have Wupa, Father, Uncle Osa, and me. Everyone loves Wupa and respects him."

"Yes," sighed Hah-nee.

"Now I must skin the rabbit and prairie dog and prepare stew with the herbs I have found," said Mother Nuva. She cut an ear from the rabbit, placed the gall bladder in it, and wrapped them in a yucca leaf. She threw the leaf in the fire to show that she was sorry they had to take the animal's life. They prayed for forgiveness. She did the same thing with the prairie dog. Hah-nee brought wood for the fire and waited for the stew to cook. It was a wonderful supper. Father and Uncle Osa were so happy over the rain and the good supper that they told all kinds of stories around the fire afterwards. They told of a forest fire they had once seen; of a woman who had three children all at once; and all about a great plague of grasshoppers years ago that ate up all the corn plants. Hah-nee took a tender piece of rabbit up to

Wupa to suck. Wupa liked it so much he belched and belched, which is the Indian custom of complimenting the cook.

Hah-nee called Mozo and the two wrapped themselves in a blanket of rabbit fur for the night. Even if Wupa and Mother Nuva had told him all would be well and he need not fear, far down in his heart he knew he was different. He did not belong to the cliff dwellers with whom he had lived most of his young life. And so he slept badly that night, in spite of Mozo and the warm blanket.

CHAPTER FOUR

HAH-NEE BECOMES A HERO

PART of Father and Uncle Osa's cornfield lay in a long narrow gully. For many years they and their fathers before them had worked on this field, building low stone walls and leveling the land in terraces, so the rain would not rush down from the higher places and wash out the corn. Often this field had a crop when other fields on the flat mesa had little corn or squash. That was why Hah-nee was never quite as hungry as some of his friends when he went to bed at night.

Now that April and May had come, everybody was busy. The boys had no time to play hoop game or shinny. They were always in the fields with their fathers, both day and night. The enemies of growing things were everywhere; foxes, field mice, crows, ravens, and rabbits; always rabbits. When the sun was hot Hah-nee brought brush to protect the growing cornstalks. All of Hah-nee's playmates were too busy to think of anything but the crop and its care.

The priests were in the kivas all the time, chanting and sacrificing, fasting and taking steam sweat baths. These were the ways to please the gods. If the gods were pleased with men, they would send down rain and the corn would grow. In July huge white clouds promised rain. But the clouds came and went day after day and no rain fell. People began to worry. They were always careful not to waste any food but now the meals grew smaller and smaller, and many were constantly hungry.

One night Hah-nee and his friend Tayu were in the brush shelter where their fields joined. Tayu was asleep. It was Hah-nee's turn to watch the field and scare away any animals of the night. The corn was not high, but ears were beginning to form.

Just before dawn the birds began their usual chirping. An owl, always the most feared of all birds by the Indians, hooted sadly, and then flew away. It seemed almost like a warning of disaster. The sky grew lighter. Hah-nee listened to the bird calls and wondered if the coming day would be as hot as all the others had been. He threw a stone and scared away a hungry crow. Feeling sleepy, he perched on a rock and gazed over the distant desert. Soon he could go home and eat.

Just then he noticed a moving mass on the desert like a dust cloud. As it came nearer he saw that the darker spots in the cloud moved, like a band of antelopes being chased by a hunter. He got his bow ready and climbed to a higher terrace where he could see better. Now the cloud was nearer and suddenly he knew that a war party of Ute Indians was on the move.

Hah-nee had often heard from Uncle Osa and Wupa stories

of nomad raids upon the farmer Indians. He knew that the Utes never raided the larger cliff dwellings. The ledges were too high. The people were too many. Sometimes the Ute warriors captured women and children at an isolated water hole. Sometimes they killed a farmer working in his field. But now Hah-nee was sure the Utes were after food, for the entire country had suffered in the drought and game was scarce.

Hah-nee ran to the brush shelter and shook his friend Tayu.

"Tayu, wake up," he cried. "The Utes are coming to raid our fields. They are still far out in the desert. There is time to spread the warning among the watchers of the lower fields. I will run to the cliff dwellings and warn the men."

Tayu grabbed his bow and arrow and hurried away. Hah-nee was a fast runner. In no time at all he spread the word of the coming invasion. People beat on sticks, rattled deer hoofs, shouted and made a great din. Soon everybody up and down the canyon knew that the enemy was coming. The men raced to their fields, armed with bows, arrows, spears, and shields. Women, children, and old men remained in the cliff homes, guarding the trails that led up or down to their dwellings.

Hah-nee raced after the men, out of breath. Each Indian thought of his own field, his own corn, his own squash. If he lost his tiny crop to the invaders, the winter might bring starvation to his family. Storage bins were already almost empty in many homes.

When Hah-nee reached his field, he could see that many cliff dwellers had run down the slopes to meet the invaders. The

warriors had now split into small bands, hoping thus to trap some of the cliff dwellers. But the farmer Indians knew every bush, every rock, every tree, every hiding place on their mesa. Before the sun was very high the hungry, disappointed warriors turned and fled back into the dusty desert, leaving on the rocky slopes of the mesa two of their dead.

The boy Hah-nee gazed upon one of the dead Utes, lying where he had been struck from behind with an arrow. His arms were spread out. He was tall, as Hah-nee was tall. His head was long and round behind. As Hah-nee looked at the dead man, he thought he might even be his older brother or his father. A strange feeling of belonging and yet not belonging came over him. He felt sad and all mixed up inside. But the cliff dwellers, joy in their hearts, turned to their precious fields, thankful for even the stunted stalks and the meager squash.

In the kivas that night and on the terraces of the City was much rejoicing. In all of the smaller cliff dwellings there was singing, chanting, beating on hollow logs, playing of flutes. There were ceremonials of joy. Hah-nee was a hero. He was the first to see the invaders. He acted quickly. He spread the alarm that saved the fields and perhaps the lives of some of the people. He was invited into the kiva of the Corn Clan and given a special bowl of food. Wupa praised him and so did Father, Mother, and Uncle Osa. Mother gave him a sweet piece of yucca jelly she had saved for just such a happy time. He was so glad and so joyous that he almost forgot the fears that had haunted him. And the fields were saved for a while at least.

CHAPTER FIVE

WUPA'S BAG

A FEW days later, as Hah-nee was returning home from all-night guard duty of the field, he noticed Kisha circling above a tall pine tree. He whistled to Kisha, but the raven would not come to his call. He was hunting a squirrel and was very busy.

As Hah-nee was about to descend the cliff, he saw something red dangling from a limb of a dwarf pine tree. The tree grew out of the solid cliff face below the rim. At first Hah-nee thought the swaying red object was a bird, then he saw it was Wupa's bag. But how could he get it? Below the rim the cliff fell hundreds of feet straight down. He might slip and break his leg on the sharp rocks below.

Hah-nee searched for a stick. He found a long forked one. Then he lay flat on the edge of the rim, reaching far out over the cliff. With the forked stick he tried to catch the bag by its red string. He tried again and again. After a long time he finally caught hold of the string. Up, up, up he pulled the bag. It *was* the bag Kisha had stolen, Wupa's precious bag.

In his excitement Hah-nee forgot he was tired and hungry. He hastened down to Wupa's home, the bag in his hands. The old man was asleep on his bearskin rug as usual. Hah-nee tiptoed over to him calling, "Grandfather, wake up."

But Wupa slept on.

"Wupa, Wupa," cried Hah-nee in his ear. Wupa opened his slits of eyes, muttering, "Oh, it's Hah-nee. What have you there? Mush for Wupa?"

"Something better than mush, Grandfather. Look."

When Wupa saw the bag he smiled happily, asking, "Where did you find this, Hah-nee?"

"I was walking over the mesa and saw Kisha circling in the sky over a tall pine tree. I whistled, but he would not come. He was after a squirrel I think. Then I saw something hanging on a little tree that grew right out of the face of the steep cliff. I found a stick and after trying a long time caught the bag on the stick and brought it up. Kisha must have carried it away to bury it somewhere, and it must have caught in the tree as he was flying upward."

"The old rascal," said Wupa. "Now I will hide the bag where he will never find it again. Do you know why I treasure the bag so much, Hah-nee?"

"Because you wove it when you were young?" answered Hah-nee.

"Yes, that, but something more. I have sacred things in this bag," replied Wupa, untying the red string.

"Sacred pollen?" asked Hah-nee.

"Of course, sacred pollen, and some other things. I will show you," said the old man. "Here is the sacred pollen in this bit of skin. Here are two red feathers from a parrot I got years and years ago when I went far to the south to get cotton for my wedding blanket."

"Oh," sighed Hah-nee, "they are beautiful." He fingered the bright red feathers.

"Here is the lightning knife. It is at the head of the lightning when it strikes a tree in a storm. It is very strong."

Hah-nee fingered the shining black stone shaped like an arrow point.

"But most of all, Hah-nee," said Wupa, "this white crystal here is the most valuable thing I have. The other things I could find again, but not this white crystal."

Hah-nee took the crystal, and as he turned it he saw how beautifully the light caught each side. "Where did you find this, Grandfather? It is like a rainbow after the storm."

"That is a crystal which I got years ago, the same time I got the parrot feathers and the two tiny shells in the bag. It was given to me by an old dear friend, Mai, who lives far to the southeast of here, many days journey. I was very young then and so was Mai. We became great friends. He had a little son only a few years old. One day the boy was playing near his father's cornfield, and he fell asleep in a little ditch. Suddenly a cloudburst sent a wall of water down the little canyon. It happened I was close by and I dragged the boy out of the muddy water just

in time. Mai never forgot. Before I left, Mai took this crystal from his bag and gave it to me saying, 'Wupa if you ever need help, or any of your clan need help, this crystal in their hands will be a symbol for me to help them.' "

Hah-nee fingered the white crystal, enjoying its rare beauty. "So you know the land to the southeast, Grandfather."

"I did know it well, but that was many years ago when I made that journey. It was a fair land then. A great river passed near the pueblo where Mai and his people live. They grow corn, but they never had the great dryness that we have had over the years. This is what I have been thinking, Hah-nee. The time will come one day, and soon, when you will see me as you saw me this morning. Asleep. But, Hah-nee, then you cannot awaken me, no matter how hard you try. I shall have gone on the long, long sleep, the sleep we all must make. But you must not be sad, for it is a good land to which I go."

Hah-nee felt very sad, for to lose Wupa would be like losing Mother Nuva. "When will that be, Grandfather?" he asked wonderingly.

"No one knows, Hah-nee. But the long sleep is near. I feel more and more as the days go by that it is near. So, before I go, Hah-nee, I have been thinking of you and your family. I have a plan."

"A plan?" asked Hah-nee.

"Hah-nee," continued the old man, "go to the corner of the room and pull out that piece of white buckskin you see there."

Hah-nee did as the old man said. He handed the buckskin

to him. Wupa unrolled it and laid it flat on the floor of the terrace. Then he said, "Now, Hah-nee, go to your room and bring back some beeweed your mother has there to paint her jars with. And a yucca-leaf brush."

When Hah-nee reached his home, no one was there. On a ledge was a fine jar Mother Nuva had been working on. It was partly decorated. Black designs on a white ground and very beautiful.

Hah-nee found a yucca-leaf brush and a bowl of black beeweed paint. He returned to Wupa's ledge. "Here is the paint and the brush," he said. "Now what are you going to do?"

Wupa did not reply. He moistened the brush and Hah-nee watched the old man's hand tremble as he placed the brush on the buckskin.

"Watch, Hah-nee. I will draw the trail I took to the home of my friend Mai. Here is our cliff dwelling. You travel along the canyon until you come to a river. Here. It may be dry now. You cross that river and then you will see high mountains. Go to the west of them. Here, right here," and he marked a dot, "you will see a spring. Beside the spring is a very old and very green tree. Then you walk for two more suns along this trail. Then you will see a huge mountain that goes up into the sky and has a sharp point like an arrow tip. Here is another spring."

Wupa's trembling hand made another dot on the buckskin. He drew and talked at the same time. "Two more suns journey to the southeast, and here is another spring. It may not be there now, for it is many years since I went that way. Here you will

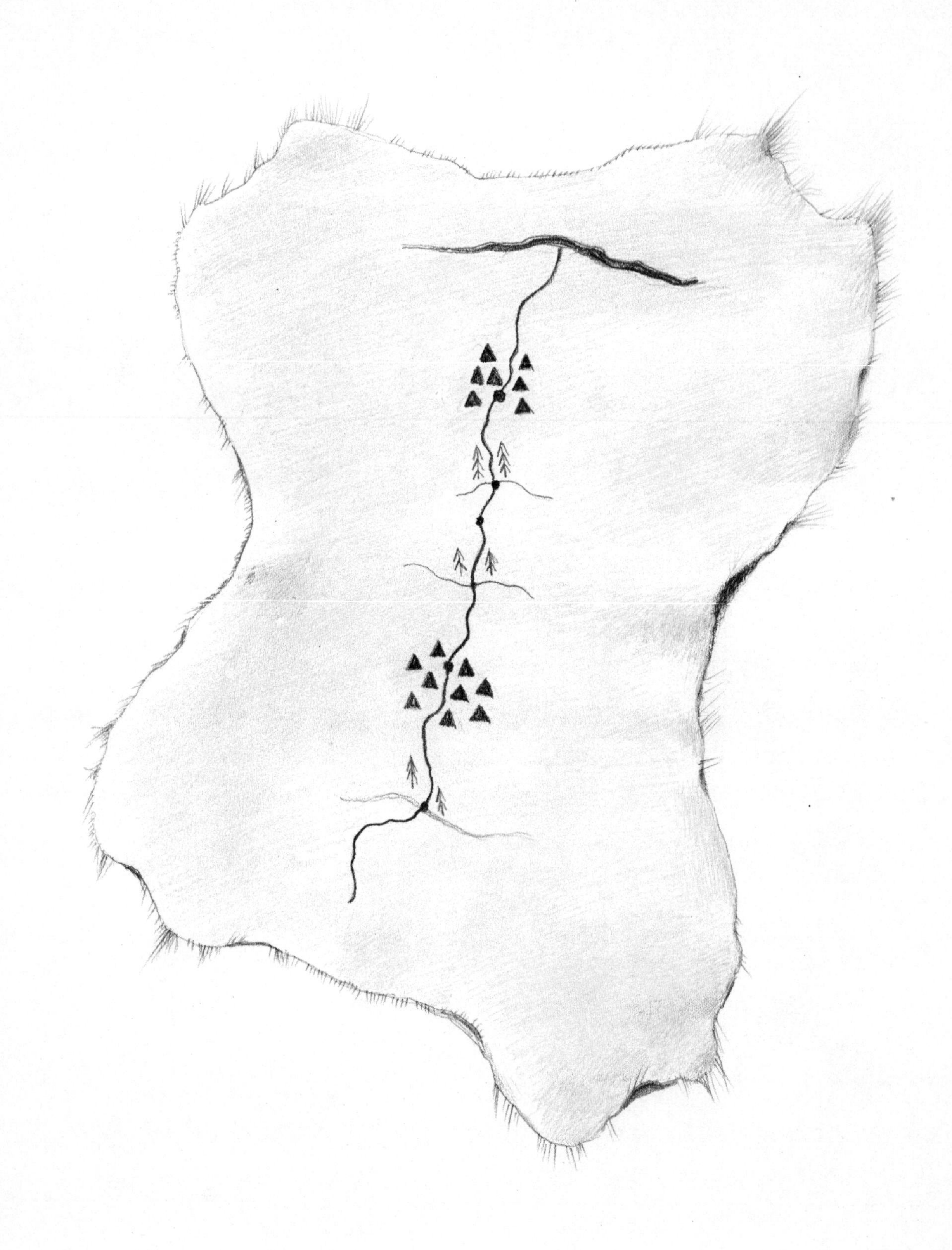

finally come to a land with stone houses by a broad flowing river. It is in a straight line as a bird flies from this place." He pointed to the last spring he had drawn on the buckskin. "In that land lives my friend Mai. He is beloved of his people. I am sure by now he is a great leader among them."

"But, Grandfather," asked Hah-nee, "why do you ask us to leave our home in the cliffs?"

"I do not know if you will leave, Hah-nee. Perhaps, perhaps not. If the crops should fail and fail and fail and no rain fall, it may be you will *want* to leave the cliffs. When I go on the long sleep, people may turn against you and your family, because you are of enemy blood. Then it may be you will want to go to the land of Mai. You know, son, when people become frightened, they do many strange things. They always try to find someone to blame for their troubles. They might think that you are causing the drought, who knows? The people of the Coyote Clan, who are jealous of our fields, may remind the priests. The priests are frantic now."

"But it *may* rain," said Hah-nee hopefully.

"Yes it *may* rain and the crops *may* be good. Then the people will forget. But if the rains do not fall, people will not forget. And because I am an old, old man and have seen many people act in many ways, I made this plan for you."

The old fear gripped Hah-nee's heart and he cried out, "I do not want to leave these cliffs, Grandfather, and I do not want to leave you and Kisha."

"I know, Hah-nee. It is hard to leave the place where one

has always lived. And to go far away to a place one does not know. But remember you have a friend in the far land who will help you. Think of the corn Father and Uncle Osa will raise. Think of the beautiful jars Mother will make, jars out of her heart and her mind. And you will make new friends, Hah-nee, and can play the hoop game and go rabbit hunting with them. And you will never go to bed hungry."

Then Hah-nee remembered Honani, she of the child's mind, and the other Indians who had been driven from the cliffs into the desert by the maddened people. They were witches. This same thing could happen to him. The priests might need to find some new evil spirit, for the drought was long. He rolled up the buckskin as Wupa said:

"Keep this skin and do not show it to anyone. Not until I have gone on the long, long sleep. Here is the crystal. Guard it well. Do not let Kisha see it. He would try to steal it again. He loves shiny things."

Hastily Hah-nee put the crystal in his bag. He rolled up the buckskin, for just at that moment Kisha swept into the cliff dwelling like a black arrow. He laid a dead squirrel before his master.

"You speak of that bird and here he is," said Wupa smiling. "Now go, my son, and eat. Do not tell any of the plan until the time is ready. Keep this secret locked in your heart. If the time comes when you must go on the long desert trail to the Land of Mai, think of Wupa. For he will be with you."

"What shall we do with Kisha?" asked Hah-nee.

"Kisha? Take him with you. Few people love him here, and

many fear him. When I am gone they might harm him. He loves me best of all, but he will love you when I am gone. He will help you on the way in finding game. He is a good hunter. For several days tie him to you, for he will want to return to find me. Then the people might think him evil and kill him. Take him with you," he continued, stroking Kisha's long black feathers as Kisha muttered his usual "Caw, caw," as if to say, "Yes, yes."

"Grandfather, I go now and take back the brush, the paint, and hide the buckskin," said Hah-nee, tears in his eyes.

"Go, Hah-nee, and do not be sad. Wupa goes to a good land. He does not fear. He has tried to live as his fathers have taught him. He goes to a land where his bones will be young again, and where his eyes can see far away. Where he can again hunt the deer, and hoe the corn."

Hah-nee climbed down to his home, hiding the buckskin under his sleeping mat. Then he sat on a rock by the fire, eating cold corn cakes and admiring Mother's beautiful jar. She will be unhappy that she cannot take it with her, he thought, but thinking of the jar made him think again of the Land of Mai. She will make many beautiful jars there, he thought. And the longer he dreamed of the journey the happier he became. The fear of the people's wrath as the drought continued had begun to burden him. So within the Indian boy's heart came the hope of knowing new places and new people, and he grew happier as he thought of the land he would soon see.

CHAPTER SIX

THE LAND OF MAI

IT WAS hard for Hah-nee to keep Wupa's secret to himself. Often he would creep into his hut when everyone was away and study the picture Wupa had painted on the buckskin. He saw the river they must cross; the cottonwood tree at the spring; the mountain with a point like an arrow. But most of all the land of the Great River. Often he took out the white crystal from his bag and enjoyed its beautiful colors. He thought of the day he would show it to Mai. And the more he dreamed of the new land the more anxious he was to go away. As the hot days dragged on he felt that the people were more and more unfriendly. Or did he only *think* so? The boys of the Coyote Clan threw rocks in his direction when he passed by their home, and called out names after him.

As August ended and the "man" rains did not come, September was just as hot. All night in the kivas the priests prayed, fasted, chanted, and used every charm they knew to try to please the gods. Nothing that they did brought the longed-for rain. The sun rose each morning hot in a cloudless sky. Much of the small game disappeared, rabbits, squirrels, mice, birds. It was hard to find even a little field mouse. People were really hungry but more than that they feared their gods had deserted them.

Early one morning as Hah-nee was returning from his all-night field duty, he climbed to Wupa's cell. Wupa lay on his bear-skin rug as usual, sound asleep. Hah-nee had seen him that way for many years. But this time when he tried to awaken him, he could not. The old man had gone on the long, long sleep he had so often wished for. Hah-nee was frightened. He called for his mother. Everyone was unhappy. Everyone was sad. But Wupa looked so peaceful lying on his bearskin that it was hard for Hah-nee to weep as did the others. He remembered what Wupa had told him, that he would be young again in the land to which he was going.

They wrapped Wupa in a cotton and feather blanket, and buried him in a shallow grave at the rear of his cell. They placed food, water, his precious bag, his bow and arrow, his tools beside him. He might need them in the world to come.

Each morning, for three days, Mother Nuva placed water and food on Wupa's grave. On the morning of the fourth day his spirit would leave his body and enter the earth through the spirit hole in the kiva.

On the morning of the third day after Wupa's death, Mother Nuva and Father and Uncle Osa became frightened. Something terrible had happened during the night. When Father went to look at his withering corn, he found two rows completely stripped of ears. All the squash was gone too. Then, when he came to tell his wife, he found her in tears. During the night someone had thrown a rock at her beautiful new jar, and it lay on the terrace in many small pieces. Everything was happening at once.

That night the family sat around their fire, thinking sadly of their cornfield and the broken jar, and Wupa's dèath. They were wondering if there would be enough corn for the winter ahead. Suddenly Hah-nee heard Tayu whistle. He slipped from the fire to the edge of the cliff.

"Hah-nee," whispered Tayu, "come. I have something to tell you."

The two boys found an abandoned storehouse and sat down in the darkness.

"Hah-nee," said Tayu, "I am your friend. I have always been your friend. We have played together and worked together always. But now I can be your friend no longer."

"Why is that, Tayu?" whispered Hah-nee, "What has happened?"

"My father forbids me to see you. He says the people say you are an enemy. They whisper that you are working with evil spirits. Some even say you are the one who has caused the long drought. Siki, that old gossip of the Coyote Clan, says the drought started when you first came here. If you go away it will rain, she says."

"She says that," exclaimed Hah-nee. "How did you learn of this?"

"My brother, who is in the kiva now, for he is to be a priest,

told me. Tomorrow it will be four days since Wupa died. His spirit enters the spirit hole in the kiva at dawn. Then, Hah-nee, if you are still here, I fear for you. You may be dragged before the council of the elders and no one knows what the council might do with you."

"Will they harm the rest of my family, do you think?"

"I do not know. But when people are afraid as they are now, it is hard to say what they will do. You remember how they chased old Honani away?"

"Yes," answered Hah-nee, his heart beating fast with fear.

"I must go now, for they might miss me. My father would be very angry if he knew I warned you."

The boy slipped quietly away in the darkness. Hah-nee sat in the storeroom for a while thinking what he should do. He was very much afraid. Perhaps this was the time to tell his family of Wupa's plan. He slipped back to the fire and sat beside his mother.

"Was that Tayu?" she asked.

"Yes," replied Hah-nee. "It was Tayu." He darted quickly into his room and returned with the buckskin in his hand. He laid it out on the stone terrace before the fire, saying, "Now the time has come that I must tell you a secret I have known for a long, long time, Wupa's secret and mine."

The three before the fire looked at the boy in wonder. He took up a stick, and as he traced the black line on the buckskin, he said, "Tayu says the people are afraid of me. Someone broke Mother's jar. Someone else stole the corn and squash. It is now as Wupa warned. He said that harm might come to us as soon as his spirit enters the new world."

"But what are you doing with that stick, Hah-nee? What is that line you are drawing on the buckskin?" asked Father.

"That is the trail we should take to the new land of Mai, Father. Wupa drew this trail on the buckskin with beeweed before he died. He has a very old friend in a land far to the southeast by the Great River, whose name is Mai." Hah-nee pointed with the stick to the bottom of the buckskin. "It is many days journey to the Land of Mai. Wupa was there when he was young. He gave me this white crystal, and said that Mai had given it to him for saving the life of his little son. Mai told Wupa years ago that he would be kind to any who bore the crystal."

Then Hah-nee explained the trail. He pointed to the river, the springs, the mountain with a point like an arrow, and the mesa by the Great River.

"And you have kept this secret for a long time, Hah-nee?" asked Father with wondering eyes.

"Yes, for a long time, Father," said Hah-nee proudly. "Wupa warned me not to say a word, for if I did the priests might learn of it. At dawn tomorrow Wupa's spirit enters the new world. After that Wupa will not be here to protect us."

"So it is," said Father in meditation.

"So it is," said Uncle Osa. "Then we must go tonight. Tonight when all are sleeping."

"I suppose we must," said Mother sadly, "although I do not wish to go."

With no more words the Indians prepared for the long journey. They gathered what little seed corn they had, and some dried corn meal. Uncle Osa filled two gourd canteens with water. Hah-nee put a pile of piñon nuts in his carrying bag. He tied Kisha to his shoulder. Kisha was sleepy and cross.

At midnight, when a new moon was still in the sky, the four Indians, followed by Mozo, crept silently down the ladders and toe holds into the canyon for the last time. They took the well-worn path down the canyon. As it turned, Mother Nuva and Hah-nee looked back at the Great City they had known always, now dark and silent in deep shadow. A fire flickered here and there against a stone wall; a turkey gobbled. The ancient cliffs. Their old home. The home they would never see again. Then they hurried after the men.

Mozo, as the trail passed under some smaller cliff dwellings, growled; so Hah-nee tied his mouth with a strong yucca fiber. They feared someone might see them slipping quietly away. Once they passed a late hunter on the trail, but they did not know him nor did he know them.

They came to the river at dawn. Not one drop of water flowed over the sand. All that day the Indian family plodded on through the heat and dust. Often they unrolled the map that Wupa had drawn on the deerskin and studied it carefully. A day later they came to the land of the high mountains and found the spring. But the old tree was gone. Two more suns and they reached the mountain with the sharp peak like an arrow but found no spring. That night, as they camped, Uncle Osa and

Father dug a deep hole in the sand. In the morning, as Hah-nee looked into the hole he saw water had seeped up from below. The Indians drank deeply of the cool water. Filling their clay jars, they stumbled on, ever southeast.

On the morning of the sixth day, a desert sandstorm suddenly blotted out sky, mountains and trail. As the hot sands swirled about them, the Indian family found refuge between great rocks. All day long they lay there trying to breathe through the wet rags over their faces. Kisha tucked his head under his wing and slept. As Hah-nee lay close to his mother, he whispered, "Mother, do you think we will EVER, EVER, get to the land of Mai? My throat and eyes hurt so." Nuva answered wearily, "I don't know, my son, we can only hope and try to keep on the trail that Wupa drew for us."

The next day they hurried along, Hah-nee, Uncle Osa, Mother Nuva and Father, each thinking his own thoughts. Mother was thinking of the beautiful jars she would make in the land to come. Father and Uncle Osa saw rows and rows of tall green corn with golden tassels, fat squash, and jars full of brown shining beans in the land of the Great River.

In the morning the air was clear and they could see for miles in every direction. Hah-nee untied the string around Kisha's leg and let him fly away to hunt for food. Several hours later he returned, a lean jack rabbit dangling from his bill. Suddenly everybody felt better. Now they knew they would have something to eat. After supper, by the light of the fire, the men made new moccasins. Their old ones were torn to shreds by sand, rocks and the sharp spines of cactus everywhere over the desert.

As the days went by, the desert began to grow more green. They came to a beautiful cottonwood tree and rested in its shade. It was wonderful to see a green tree again. Then they walked on and on until it was quite dark. Camping in a deep sandy gully, they were so tired that they slept all through the night.

Before dawn Hah-nee was awakened by the sound of rustling leaves. Was he dreaming of the cornfields of home? Then he heard the faint sound of an Indian flute. He climbed hastily up the sandy ravine. As he stood in the dim light of dawn he could not believe what he saw. Before him was a vast field of corn, the green leaves rustling in the wind. Beyond the cornfield rose a great rocky mesa.

They had reached the Land of Mai.

And Hah-nee, as he held tight to Kisha's leash, thought often of Wupa, whose spirit and faith he felt with him. He thought of the friends he was leaving, especially Tayu; of the sweet sound of the flute player welcoming the sun. He was wondering whom he would play with in the land of Mai. Would Mai have a grandson? What would Mai look like? But most of all for Hah-nee, the sorrows and fears of the past month began to fade away. He would make new friends. No one would call him FUNNYHEAD or UTE. He would be the son of Nuva, come from the far-off land of the Northwest, the land of the Cliff Dwellers.

EPILOGUE

Thus
Went Hah-nee and his family
Into the wilderness
As others had gone
Before them

Days of wandering
Days of hunger and thirst
Days of danger
Lay before Hah-nee and his family
Until they reached the distant land
The land of Mai.
The land of a flowing river
The Great Rio Grande

There
Upon a broad mesa
They found friends
They built a new home
The land grew high with corn
And they were content

So it was with many other
Dwellers of the cliffs

As the years of drought dragged on
Twenty-four long years.

The cliff cities of the canyons
Of the Great Southwest
Slowly fell to ruin

Only the owl hooted there
As the rat scurried in and out
And the wind whined about empty homes
For the people had gone
To mingle with other peoples far to the south
Leaving their ancient homes
Forever

And today
As one stumbles through the dust
Of silent rooms
And peers into the empty kivas
Where once priests prayed for rain
One lives again
That ancient life
Forgotten for six hundred years
The life of Hah-nee
Of the Cliff Country